PUFFIN BOOKS
THE PUFFIN BOOK OF POETRY
FOR CHILDREN

Eunice de Souza was born in Poona, and educated in Bombay and the US. For many years she lectured at St Xavier's College, Bombay, where she retired as the Head of the Department of English in 2000. She has published four books of poems, two novellas, several anthologies and books for children. Eunice lives in Bombay.

Melanie Silgardo was born and educated in Bombay. She has published two books of poetry and was a founder-member of a poetry publishing house, Newground, also in Bombay. She has worked in publishing, both in India and in the UK, where she worked with Virago Press for many years. She has edited anthologies of poetry and short fiction. Melanie lives in London.

The Puffin Book of Poetry for Children
for Children
101 Poems

Edited by
Eunice de Souza and Melanie Silgardo

PUFFIN BOOKS

PUFFIN BOOKS
Published by the Penguin Group
Penguin Books India Pvt. Ltd, 11 Community Centre, Panchsheel Park, New
Delhi 110 017, India
Penguin Group (USA) Inc., 375 Hudson Street, New York, New York 10014,
USA
Penguin Group (Canada), 90 Eglinton Avenue East, Suite 700, Toronto,
Ontario, M4P 2Y3, Canada (a division of Pearson Penguin Canada Inc.)
Penguin Books Ltd, 80 Strand, London WC2R 0RL, England
Penguin Ireland, 25 St Stephen's Green, Dublin 2, Ireland (a division of
Penguin Books Ltd)
Penguin Group (Australia), 250 Camberwell Road, Camberwell, Victoria
3124, Australia (a division of Pearson Australia Group Pty Ltd)
Penguin Group (NZ), cnr Airborne and Rosedale Roads, Albany, Auckland
1310, New Zealand (a division of Pearson New Zealand Ltd)
Penguin Group (South Africa) (Pty) Ltd, 24 Sturdee Avenue, Rosebank,
Johannesburg 2196, South Africa

Penguin Books Ltd, Registered Offices: 80 Strand, London WC2R 0RL, England

First published by Penguin Books India 2005

This anthology copyright © Eunice de Souza and Melanie Silgardo 2005
Introduction copyright © Eunice de Souza and Melanie Silgardo 2005
Pages 98–103 (Acknowledgements) constitute an extension of the copyright page

10 9 8 7 6 5 4 3 2 1

For sale in the Indian Subcontinent only

ISBN-10: 0143 335960
ISBN-13: 9781433359606

Typeset by Eleven Arts, New Delhi
Printed at Pauls Press, New Delhi

Contents

Introduction

Dear Readers

If you can get at least half the pleasure reading this volume as it has given us putting it together for you, we will have achieved what we set out to do.

Many of the poems here are old familiars, reading and rereading them have made them old friends over the years. We want you to meet them and know them as well as we do. They may seem strange at first, but let them in, for they may have unexpected gifts for you.

How do poems work, and what makes them so pleasing to read, even when we don't immediately understand what is going on? Part of the pleasure is that they are mysterious jewels that glint a little more, or differently, every time you read them. You discover a new facet; the jewel becomes a little more valuable. The delight of reading, and of reading poetry especially, is that for a small short space we get into the heart and mind of another person—a person who may have lived many years ago, or one who lives very far away, in another country, and who speaks a different language—but who talks to us across this distance. And what is more, through the magic of poetry we understand them. They have something to tell us and we listen carefully.

There are poems that make you think: about friendship and growing up; ones about the very act of writing; poems about parents, about animals and the environment; about the cruelty of being different and being judged for it; and sad poems about losing someone close. Then there are poems that make you laugh: fun poems and nonsense poems. What we wanted to share with you was the excitement of finding poems that will leap up from the page and, sometimes whisper, sometimes shout in your ears. Some of the poems you will find difficult, and they may just rest for a while on the page, until the next time you read them. That is also what is special about poetry—that you need to work at it a little bit, and discover your relationship with it.

Try and read these poems aloud. Poetry often works much better when you hear it. You will notice even when it doesn't rhyme (a lot of modern poetry doesn't, and is written in 'free verse') there is a rhythm and an internal form that makes it different from prose broken up into short lines. So read the poems aloud with friends, or get your parents to read them aloud to you. The poems are arranged in a completely random way—alphabetically according to the poet's names—thus ensuring an element of surprise where they fall. We decided against organizing them by theme, country of origin, or the time when they were written. We wanted you to happen upon them by chance and respond to them spontaneously.

Perhaps some of you will be inspired to write poems yourselves. There are a few poems in this volume that have been written by children your age. They write about things that touched them or they have observed. Look around you, the streets and skies are full of material to write about. Poems are plucked from the air we breathe, and the sights we see, and the emotions we feel. We cannot all be writers, but happily we can all be readers, turning these poems as they glint and sparkle, discovering treasures as we go along. Enjoy!

Eunice de Souza

July 2005   Melanie Silgardo

For a Five Year Old

Fleur Adcock

A snail is climbing up the window sill
Into your room, after a night of rain.
You call me in to see, and I explain
That it would be unkind to leave it there:
It might crawl to the floor; we must take care
That no one squashes it. You understand,
And carry it outside, with careful hand,
To eat a daffodil.

I see, then, that a kind of faith prevails:
Your gentleness is moulded still by words
From me, who have trapped mice and shot wild birds,
From me, who drowned your kittens, who betrayed
Your closest relatives, and who purveyed
The harshest kind of truth to many another.
But that is how things are: I am your mother,
And we are kind to snails.

Rat Race

John Agard

Rat race?
Don't make us laugh.
It's you humans
who're always in a haste.

Ever seen a rat
in a bowler hat
rushing to catch a train?

Ever seen a rat
with a briefcase
hurrying through the rain?

And isn't it a fact
that all that hurry-hurry
gives you humans heart attacks?

No, my friend,
we rats relax.

Pass the cheese,
please.

Women on the Road to Lhasa

Deepa Agarwal

Beneath the mask
my face melts
like a jaggery cake in the sun
Mercifully
I can see
even
as I preserve the pink of my skin.

But what's the use?
my sisters remain strangers
behind yak hide cheeks
that cannot exchange smiles
to lighten
the tyranny
of the road to Lhasa. All
blinding earth and searing sky
bleached bone and rubble
hung over a chafing saddle
feeding fleas.

Only
when night's black tent
enfolds the enemy, sun
can I breathe. Let
chilly air soothe broiling skin
let laughter flow free,
as
I shed the mask.

Hard it is for a woman
far from home. And
endless the road to Lhasa
beneath a mask.

Note: In *Lost World Tibet*, Amaury de Riencourt mentions that while travelling, wealthy Tibetan women wore painted face masks of yak hide to protect their complexions from the sun.

Celebrations

Ishan Agarwal

Some celebrations are nice,
Some aren't.
Weddings aren't.
An old—more like ancient—relative
Comes up to you.
'Do you remember me?
The last time I saw you
Was when you were a day old.'
But the food's nice.

Birthdays aren't that bad,
Excepting the ones with dances,
Or those with a volunteer, short magician
Who thinks he's nice
In giving people chances
To do magic.

I hate over-enthusiastic hosts
Good food and quiet guests are the best.

I like anniversaries
A card's enough.

Palestinians

Eli Alon

He returned to the desolate hill, where his village stood,
thirty years after it had been destroyed:
'The well was here, people drew water here . . .
and the house was there . . . also the fig tree . . .'
I thought of Ein Shemer, where I was born and bred,
my children too. I visualized, thirty years ahead,
the return of my son as an exile, a refugee.
His whisper came to me.
'The children's house stood here . . .
here was the dinner hall . . . I used to walk this lane,
my father's hand in mine . . . here was the lawn,
where we would play until the dark came on.
But where has everything now disappeared?
Where has everyone been dispersed?'

On Ageing

Maya Angelou

When you see me sitting quietly,
Like a sack left on the shelf,
Don't think I need your chattering.
I'm listening to myself.
Hold! Stop! Don't pity me!
Hold! Stop your sympathy!
Understanding if you got it,
Otherwise I'll do without it!

5

When my bones are stiff and aching
And my feet won't climb the stairs,
I will only ask one favour:
Don't bring me no rocking chair.

When you see me walking, stumbling,
Don't study and get it wrong.
'Cause tired don't mean lazy
And every goodbye ain't gone.
I'm the same person I was back then,
A little less hair, a little less chin,
A lot less lungs and much less wind,
But ain't I lucky I can still breathe in.

The Three Ravens

Anon

There were three ravens sat on a tree,
Downe a downe, hay downe, hay downe,
There were three ravens sat on a tree,
With a downe,
There were three ravens sat on a tree,
They were as blacke as they might be.
With a downe derrie, derrie, derrie, downe, downe.

The one of them said to his mate,
'Where shall we our breakfast take?'

'Downe in yonder greene field,
There lies a knight slain under his shield.

'His hounds they lie downe at his feete,
So well they can their master keepe.

'His haukes they fly so eagerly,
There's no fowle dare him come nie.'

Downe there comes a fallow doe,
As great with yong as she might goe.

She lift up his bloudy hed,
And kist his wounds that were so red.

She got him up upon her backe,
And carried him to earthen lake.

She buried him before the prime,
She was dead herself ere evensong time.

God send every gentleman
Such haukes, such hounds, and such a leman.

Prayer

Anon

'Lord! Let me catch a fish
So large that even I,
In telling of it afterwards,
Shall have no need to lie.'

The Common Cormorant

Anon

The common cormorant or shag
Lays eggs inside a paper bag
The reason you will see, no doubt,
It is to keep the lightning out.
But what these unobservant birds
Have never noticed is that herds
Of wandering bears may come with buns
And steal the bags to hold the crumbs.

Night Mail

W.H. Auden

This is the Night Mail crossing the border,
Bringing the cheque and the postal order,
Letters for the rich, letters for the poor,
The shop at the corner and the girl next door.
Pulling up Beattock, a steady climb:
The gradient's against her, but she's on time.
Past cotton grass and moorland boulder
Shovelling white steam over her shoulder,
Snorting noisily as she passes
Silent miles of wind-bent grasses.

Birds turn their heads as she approaches,
Stare from the bushes at her blank-faced coaches.
Sheepdogs cannot turn her course;
They slumber on with paws across.
In the farm she passes no one wakes,
But a jug in the bedroom gently shakes.

Dawn freshens, the climb is done.
Down towards Glasgow she descends
Towards the steam tugs yelping down the glade of cranes,
Towards the fields of apparatus, the furnaces
Set on the dark plain like gigantic chessmen.
All Scotland waits for her:
In the dark glens, beside the pale-green sea lochs
Men long for news.

Letters of thanks, letters from banks,
Letters of joy from the girl and the boy,
Receipted bills and invitations
To inspect new stock or visit relations,
And applications for situations
And timid lovers' declarations
And gossip, gossip from all the nations,
News circumstantial, news financial,
Letters with holiday snaps to enlarge in,
Letters with faces scrawled in the margin,
Letters from uncles, cousins and aunts,
Letters to Scotland from the South of France,
Letters of condolence to Highlands and Lowlands
Notes from overseas to Hebrides
Written on paper of every hue,
The pink, the violet, the white and the blue,
The chatty, the catty, the boring, adoring,
The cold and official and the heart's outpouring,
Clever, stupid, short and long,
The typed and the printed and the spelt all wrong.

Thousands are still asleep
Dreaming of terrifying monsters,
Or of friendly tea beside the band at Cranston's or Crawford's:
Asleep in working Glasgow, asleep in well-set Edinburgh,
Asleep in granite Aberdeen,
They continue their dreams,

And shall wake soon and long for letters,
And none will hear the postman's knock
Without a quickening of the heart,
For who can bear to feel himself forgotten?

A Parent's/Child's Poem

Jimmy P. Avasia

Brush your teeth each night
And do not enter where your dreams stray.
Pretend you never saw them and awake
More dutiful each happy day.

If there's anything to be said, I'll tell you,
Anything worth hearing, you will hear,
Anything worth giving, I will sell you.

Keep away from the world, you cannot trust it
Parents are the only ones that care
And if you find their responses rusted,
Appreciate at least that they are there.

Forgive your parents, you cannot understand them
They have their hang-ups hung up for you to see
Almost as if you'd planned them.

When you need a hand
And they give you a glove
You will know your dependence
From your love.

Cat

Rex Baker

I had an antisocial cat,
A scabby beast that scratched and spat.
He'd prowl the alley, snarl and fight,
A horrid vandal, dark as night.

His lack of virtue made me sad,
His savage howling drove me mad.
I couldn't stand his anguished whine,
The angry arching of his spine.

I grabbed the creature by its back
And stuffed it in a canvas sack,
Then hurled it from the riverbank;
The cat swam off, the sack just sank.

How Do I Love Thee?

Elizabeth Barrett Browning

How do I love thee? Let me count the ways.
I love thee to the depth and breadth and height
My soul can reach, when feeling out of sight
For the ends of Being and ideal Grace.

I love thee to the level of everyday's
Most quiet need, by sun and candlelight.
I love thee freely, as men strive for Right;
I love thee purely, as they turn from Praise.

I love thee with the passion put to use
In my old griefs, and with my childhood's faith.
I love thee with a love I seemed to lose
With my lost saints,—I love thee with the breath,
Smiles, tears, of all my life!—and, if God choose,
I shall but love thee better after death.

The Tyger

William Blake

Tyger! Tyger! burning bright
In the forests of the night,
What immortal hand or eye
Could frame thy fearful symmetry?

In what distant deeps or skies
Burnt the fire of thine eyes?
On what wings dare he aspire?
What the hand dare seize the fire?

And what shoulder, and what art,
Could twist the sinews of thy heart?
And when thy heart began to beat,
What dread hand, and what dread feet?

What the hammer? what the chain?
In what furnace was thy brain?
What the anvil? what dread grasp
Dare its deadly terrors clasp?

When the stars threw down their spears,
And water'd heaven with their tears,
Did he smile his work to see?
Did he who make the Lamb make thee?

Tyger! Tyger! burning bright
In the forests of the night,
What immortal hand or eye,
Dare frame thy fearful symmetry?

to My Brother

In memory of 1 July 1916

Vera Brittain

Your battle-wounds are scars upon my heart,
Received when in that grand and tragic 'show'
You played your part
Two years ago.

And silver in the summer morning sun
I see the symbol of your courage glow—
That Cross you won
Two years ago.

Though now again you watch the shrapnel fly,
And hear the guns that daily louder grow,
As in July
Two years ago,

May you endure to lead the Last Advance
And with your men pursue the flying foe
As once in France
Two years ago.

The Soldier

Rupert Brooke

If I should die, think only this of me:
That there's some corner of a foreign field
That is forever England. There shall be
In that rich earth a richer dust concealed;
A dust whom England bore, shaped, made aware,
Gave, once, her flowers to love, her ways to roam;
A body of England's, breathing English air,
Washed by the rivers, blest by suns of home,

And think, this heart, all evil shed away,
A pulse in the eternal mind, no less
Gives somewhere back the thoughts of England given;
Her sights and sounds; dreams happy as her day;
And laughter, learnt of friends; and gentleness,
In hearts at peace, under an English heaven.

Pippa's Song

Robert Browning

The year's at the spring
And day's at the morn;
Morning's at seven;
The hillside's dew-pearled;
The lark's on the wing;
The snail's on the thorn;
God's in His heaven—
All's right with the world.

So, We'll Go No More A-roving

George Gordon Lord Byron

So, we'll go no more a-roving
So late into the night,
Though the heart be still as loving,
And the moon be still as bright.

For the sword outwears its sheath,
And the soul wears out the breast,
And the heart must pause to breathe,
And love itself have rest.

Though the night was made for loving,
And the day returns too soon,
Yet we'll go no more a-roving
By the light of the moon.

Jabberwocky

Lewis Carroll

'Twas brillig, and the slithy toves
    Did gyre and gimble in the wabe;
All mimsy were the borogoves,
    And the mome raths outgrabe.

'Beware the Jabberwock, my son!
    The jaws that bite, the claws that catch!
Beware the Jubjub bird, and shun
    The frumious Bandersnatch!'

He took his vorpal sword in hand:
    Long time the manxome foe he sought—
So rested he by the Tumtum tree,
    And stood awhile in thought.

And, as in uffish thought he stood,
    The Jabberwock, with eyes of flame,
Came whiffling through the tulgey wood,
    And burbled as it came!

One, two! One, two! And through and through
    The vorpal blade went snicker-snack!
He left it dead, and with its head
    He went galumphing back.

'And hast thou slain the Jabberwock?
    Come to my arms, my beamish boy!
O frabjous day! Callooh! Callay!'
    He chortled in his joy.

'Twas brillig, and the slithy toves
    Did gyre and gimble in the wabe;
All mimsy were the borogoves,
    And the mome raths outgrabe.

What Has Happened to Lulu?

Charles Causley

What has happened to Lulu, mother?
What has happened to Lu?
There's nothing in her bed but an old rag doll
And by its side a shoe.

Why is her window wide, mother,
The curtain flapping free,
And only a circle on the dusty shelf
Where her money box used to be?

Why do you turn your head, mother,
And why do the teardrops fall?
And why do you crumple that note on the fire
 And say it is nothing at all?

I woke to voices late last night,
I heard an engine roar.
Why do you tell me the things I heard
Were a dream and nothing more?

I heard somebody cry, mother,
In anger or in pain.
But now I ask you why, mother,
You say it was a gust of rain.

Why do you wander about as though
You don't know what to do?
What has happened to Lulu, mother?
What has happened to Lu?

Peacock

Harindranath Chattopadhyaya

I sit and watch a silver blotch
On yonder lonely hill.
The tinkling air grows grey and bare,
The wind blows wet and chill.

The peacock dons his blue and bronze
And under the falling shower,
Spreads out his plumes and swiftly blooms
To an enamelled flower.

The Devil

Samuel Taylor Coleridge

From his brimstone bed at the break of day
A walking the Devil is gone
To visit his snug little farm, the earth,
And see how his stock goes on.

Over the hill and over the dale,
And he went over the plain,
And backwards and forwards he switched his long tail
As a gentleman switches his cane.

And how then was the Devil dressed?
Oh! He was in his Sunday best:
His jacket was red and his breeches were blue
And there was a hole where the tail came through.

All Souls' Night

Frances Cornford

My love came back to me
Under the November tree
Shelterless and dim.
He put his hand upon my shoulder,
He did not think me strange or older,
Nor I, him.

in Just-/ spring

e.e. cummings

in Just-
spring   when the world is mud-
luscious the little
lame balloonman

whistles   far   and wee

and eddieandbill come
running from marbles and
piracies and it's
spring

when the world is puddle-wonderful

the queer
old balloonman whistles
far   and   wee
and bettyandisbel comedancing

from hop-scotch and jump-rope and

it's
spring
and

          the

                    goat-footed

          balloonMan   whistles
far
and
wee

No, Sir, I Do Not Wish to Remain in the USA

Charmayne D'Souza

They never told us
This was not home,
But we knew it well
And did not need to be told:
The crows cawing
On banyan trees,
Swifting us home even now;
The monsoon drops
Democratically marking
Every human body,
Knowing that we all counted,
Important enough
For the rain to fall
Upon us,
The sun to evenly brown us.

The man at the embassy
Never told us
That stronger
Than any multiple re-entry
Visa
Was a strange emptiness
Of heart
That would nudge us
Back to where we came from—
Where the people alive
Were no worse off
Than the dying,
Only warmer.

What sleight of hand
Was there to hold us here?
The magic no longer held,
The hat was empty of promises
And rabbits;
Our souls had been cut
In half.

It was time we returned
Before we became invisible,
Time we came back home
And broke the spell,

Back then to our own
Indian rope tricks
Which had held us ensnared
All those years,
Yet promised us
Their own tortuous path
To heaven.

Homecoming

Bruce Dawe

All day, day after day, they're bringing them home,
they're picking them up, those they can find, and bringing
    them home,
they're bringing them in, piled on the hulls of Grants, in
    trucks, in convoys,
they're zipping them up in green plastic bags,
they're tagging them now in Saigon, in the mortuary coolness
they're giving them names, they're rolling them out of
the deep-freeze lockers—on the tarmac at Tan Son Nhut
the noble jets are whining like hounds,
they are bringing them home
—curly heads, kinky hairs, crew cuts, balding non-coms
—they're high, now, high and higher, over the land,
the steaming *chow mein*,

their shadows are tracing the blue curve of the Pacific
with sorrowful quick fingers, heading south, heading east,
home, home, home—and the coasts swing upward,
the old ridiculous curvatures
of earth, the knuckled hills, the mangrove swamps, the desert
     emptiness . . .
in their sterile housing they tilt towards these like skiers
—taxiing in, on the long runways, the howl of their
     homecoming rises
surrounding them like their last moments (the mash, the
     splendour)
then fading at length as they move
on to cities in whose wide web of suburbs
telegrams tremble like leaves from a wintering tree
and the spider grief swings in his bitter geometry
—they're bringing them home, now, too late, too early.

Kiph

Walter de la Mare

My Uncle Ben, who's been
To Bisk, Bhir, Biak—
Been, and come back:
To Tab, Tau, Tze, and Tomsk,
And home, by Teneriffe:
Who, brown as desert sand,
Gaunt, staring, slow and stiff,
Has chased the Unicorn
And Hippogriff,
Gave me a smooth, small, shining stone,
Called *Kiph*.

'Look'ee, now, Nevvy mine,'
He told me—'*If*
You'd wish a wish,
Just rub this smooth, small, shining stone,
Called *Kiph*.'

Hide it did I,
In a safe, secret spot;
Slept, and the place
In dreams forgot.

One wish *alone*
Now's mine: Oh, if
That stone called *Kiph*!

27

From Pahari Parrots

Eunice de Souza

V

Spring, and the trees are translucent.
One can hardly tell
leaf from parrot
berries from beak
red splash on wing
from veins that tingle.

VI

Two trees—and a garbage heap.
The garbage brings the barbets.
The parrots love the peepul tree.
There's a bulbul singing in the ashoka.
Throw in sparrows, crows and mynahs,
you have your common city garden
complete with pandemonium at dawn.

The lady on the third floor says
We should cut down the trees
she can't sleep for the noise.

Lady, you're a fingernail
scratching a blackboard.

I'm Nobody! Who Are You?

Emily Dickinson

I'm nobody! Who are you?
Are you nobody, too?
Then there's a pair of us—don't tell!
They'd advertise—you know!

How dreary to be somebody!
How public like a frog
To tell one's name the livelong day
To an admiring bog!

Near Hastings

Toru Dutt

Near Hastings, on the shingle-beach,
We loitered at the time
When ripens on the wall the peaches,
The autumn's lovely prime.
Far off,—the sea and sky seemed blent,
The day was wholly done,
The distant town its murmurs sent,
Strangers,—we were alone.

We wandered slow; sick, weary, faint,
Then one of us sat down,

No nature hers, to make complaint,—
The shadows deepened brown.
A lady past,—she was not young,
But oh! her gentle face
No painter-poet ever sung,
Or saw such saintlike grace.

She past us,—then she came again,
Observing at a glance
That we were strangers; one, in pain,—
Then asked,—were we from France?
We talked awhile,—some roses red
That seemed as wet with tears,
She gave my sister, and she said,
'God bless you both, my dears!'

Sweet were the roses,—sweet and full,
And large as lotus flowers
That in our own wide tanks we cull
To deck our Indian bowers.
But sweeter was the love that gave
Those flowers to one unknown,
I think that he who came to save
The gift a debt will own.

The lady's name I do not know,
Her face no more may see,
But yet, oh yet I love her so!
Blest, happy, may she be!
Her memory will not depart,
Though grief my years should shade,
Still bloom her roses in my heart!
And they shall never fade!

Macavity: The Mystery Cat

T.S. Eliot

Macavity's a Mystery Cat: he's called the Hidden Paw
For he's the master criminal who can defy the Law.
He's the bafflement of Scotland Yard, the Flying Squad's despair:
For when they reach the scene of crime—*Macavity's not there!*

Macavity, Macavity, there's no one like Macavity,
He's broken every human law, he breaks the law of gravity.
His powers of levitation would make a fakir stare,
And when you reach the scene of crime—*Macavity's not there!*
You may seek him in the basement, you may look up in the air
But I tell you once and once again, *Macavity's not there!*

Macavity's a ginger cat, he's very tall and thin;
You would know him if you saw him, for his eyes are sunken in.
His brow is deeply lined with thought, his head is highly domed;

His coat is dusty from neglect, his whiskers are uncombed.
He sways his head from side to side, with movements like
    a snake;
And when you think he's half asleep, he's always wide awake.

Macavity, Macavity, there's no one like Macavity,
For he's a fiend in feline shape, a monster of depravity.
You may meet him in a by-street, you may see him in the square
But when a crime's discovered, then *Macavity's not there!*

He's outwardly respectable. (They say he cheats at cards.)
And his footprints are not found in any file of Scotland Yard's.
And when the larder's looted, or the jewel case is rifled,
Or when the milk is missing, or another Peke's been stifled,
Or the greenhouse glass is broken, and the trellis past repair—
Ay, there's the wonder of the thing! *Macavity's not there!*

And when the Foreign Office find a Treaty's gone astray,
Or the Admiralty lose some plans and drawings by the way,
There may be a scrap of paper in the hall or on the stair—
But it's useless to investigate—*Macavity's not there!*
And when the loss has been disclosed, the Secret Service say:
'It *must* have been Macavity!'—but he's a mile away.
You'll be sure to find him resting, or a-licking of his thumbs,
Or engaged in doing complicated long division sums.

Macavity, Macavity, there's no one like Macavity,
There never was a Cat of such deceitfulness and suavity.
He always has an alibi, and one or two to spare:
At whatever time the deed took place—MACAVITY WASN'T
THERE!
And they say that all the Cats whose wicked deeds are
widely known
(I might mention Mungojerrie, I might mention Griddlebone)
Are nothing more than agents for the Cat who all the time
Just controls their operations: the Napoleon of Crime!

Injection

Kavita Ezekiel

Mother said:
Ingratitude is when you
Scream
During an injection
Even when ice and ether
Are applied to numb the part.

Children are ungrateful,
No matter what you do for them.
The deep freeze in the refrigerator
Is so small, there's no room
For stupid things—like ice!

My ears did not register
These complaints. Perhaps
Ice and ether had performed
Their function in the wrong area.
Everything felt numb, except
The part for the injection.

Father intervened:
Let her express herself.
If she feels better
When she screams,
Let her go ahead and
Scream.

Mother said, as often:
You're spoiling the children.
They must learn to bear pain,
Not to fuss. She uttered
The familiar truths.
Why don't you spend
More time with your daughter
If you love her so much?

From Adam Alarmed in Paradise

Manmohan Ghose

Though thou hear afar
Rattle sounds of fear
And mad impious war
Make the world one tear,

Though for sounds of slaughter
Thou this tranquil eve—
Red earth, crimson water—
Scarce in God believe;

Turn and seek in nature
His prime lovely feat,
Lose, forget the creature,
Seek his footprints sweet.

Picnic in Jammu

Zulfikar Ghose

Uncle Ayub swung me round and round
till the horizon became a rail
banked high upon the Himalayas.
The trees signalled me past. I whistled,
shut my eyes through tunnels of the air.
The family laughed, watching me puff
out my muscles, healthily aggressive.

This was late summer, before the snows
come to Kashmir, this was picnic time.

Then, uncoupling me from the sky, he
plunged me into the river, himself
a bough with me dangling at its end.
I went purple as a plum. He reared
back and lowered the branch of his arm
to grandma who swallowed me with a kiss.
Laughter peeled away my goose pimples.

This was late summer, before the snows
come to Kashmir, this was picnic time.

After we'd eaten, he aimed grapes at
my mouth. I flung at him the shells of
pomegranates and ran off. He tracked
me down the riverbank. We battled,
melon rind and apple core in our arms.
'You two!' grandma cried. 'Stop fighting, you'll
tire yourselves to death!' We didn't listen.

This was late summer, before the snows
come to Kashmir and end children's games.

I Am Becoming My Mother

Lorna Goodison

Yellow/brown woman
fingers smelling always of onions

My mother raises rare blooms
and waters them with tea
her birth waters sang like rivers
my mother is now me

My mother had a linen dress
the colour of the sky
and stored lace and damask
tablecloths
to pull shape out of her eye

I am becoming my mother
brown/yellow woman
fingers smelling always of onions

L'Enfant Glacé

Harry Graham

When Baby's cries grew hard to bear
I popped him in the Frigidaire.
I never would have done so if
I'd known that he'd be frozen stiff.
My wife said: 'George, I'm so unhappé!
Our darling's now completely *frappé*!'

Children Going to School

Hem Hemal
Translated by Michael James Hutt

Do not ask these little children,
coming toward you all in a line,
do not ask them where they are going.
They have their own roads to travel,
their own tools for creating themselves.

They have feet you cannot see,
do not ask about when and where,
these children are their own open sky,
their wings they make themselves.

Their language is different, meanings diverge,
if they are noisy, it does not matter.
Do not try to understand what they say:
these are the books of tomorrow's Nepal.

The Pulley

George Herbert

When God at first made Man,
    Having a glass of blessings standing by—
Let us (said He) pour on him all we can;
Let the world's riches, which dispersed lie,
    Contract into a span.

    So strength first made a way,
Then beauty flow'd, then wisdom, honour, pleasure:
When almost all was out, God made a stay,
Perceiving that, alone of all His treasure,
    Rest in the bottom lay.

    For if I should (said He)
Bestow this jewel also on My creature,
He would adore My gifts instead of Me,
And rest in Nature, not the God of Nature:
    So both should losers be.

    Yet let him keep the rest,
But keep them with repining restlessness;
Let him be rich and weary, that at least,
If goodness lead him not, yet weariness
    May toss him to My breast.

Impossibilities: To His Friend

Robert Herrick

My faithful friend, if you can see
The Fruit to grow up, or the Tree:
If you can see the colour come
Into the blushing Pear, or Plum:
If you can see the water grow
To cakes of Ice, or flakes of Snow:
If you can see that drop of rain
Lost in the wild sea, once again:
If you can see, how Dreams do creep
Into the Brain by easy sleep:
Then there is hope that you may see
Her love me once, who now hates me.

A Boy's Head

Miroslav Holub
Translated by Ian Milner

In it there is a spaceship
and a project
for doing away with piano lessons.

And there is
Noah's ark,
which shall be first.

And there is
an entirely new bird,
an entirely new hare,
an entirely new bumblebee.

There is a river
that flows upwards.

There is a multiplication table.
And there is anti-matter.
And it just cannot be trimmed.

I believe
that only what can be trimmed
is a head.

There is much promise
in the circumstance
that so many people have heads.

Spring and Fall

To a Young Child

Gerard Manley Hopkins

Margaret, are you grieving
Over Goldengrove unleaving?
Leaves, like the things of man, you
With your fresh thoughts care for, can you?

Ah! as the heart grows older
It will come to such sights colder
By and by, nor spare a sigh
Though worlds of wanwood leafmeal lie;
And yet you will weep and know why.
Now no matter, child, the name:
Sorrow's springs are the same.

Nor mouth had, no nor mind, expressed
What heart heard of, ghost guessed:
It is the blight man was born for,
It is Margaret you mourn for.

Amelia Mixed the Mustard

A.E. Housman

Amelia mixed the mustard,
She mixed it good and thick;
She put it in the custard
And made her mother sick.
And showing satisfaction
By many a loud huzza,
'Observe,' said she, 'the action
of mustard on Mamma.'

Be Like the Bird

Victor Hugo

Be like the bird, who,
Resting in his flight
On a twig too slight,
Feels it bend beneath him,
Yet sings,
Knowing he has wings.

Made for Each Other

Mamta Kalia

How close we felt
Discussing our dislikes,
Sharing a few hatreds,
Comparing notes about enemies.
I was elated to find
You couldn't stand *The Faery Queen*,
Dahi vadas and arranged marriages.
And you were delighted to see me
In an ill-fitting kurta,
A fag and minus-four glasses.
You said you hated pretty girls:
They were dull, silly and egoistic.
I said, 'Boys, they are horrors,
They grow sideburns and weigh so little.'
You said, 'Let's get married
And damn the world.'

The Boy Who Ran Away

John Keats

There was a naughty boy,
And a naughty boy was he.
He ran away to Scotland
The people for to see—
    Then he found that the ground
    Was as hard,
    That a yard
    Was as long,
    That a song
    Was as merry,
    That a cherry
    Was as red—
    That lead
    Was as weighty,
    That fourscore
    Was as eighty,
    That a door
    Was as wooden
    As in England—
So he stood in his shoes
    And he wonder'd,
    He wonder'd
He stood in his
    Shoes and he wonder'd.

Trees

Joyce Kilmer

I think that I shall never see
A poem lovely as a tree.

A tree whose hungry mouth is prest
Against the earth's sweet-flowing breast;

A tree that looks at God all day
And lifts her leafy arms to pray.

A tree that may in Summer wear
A nest of robins in her hair;

Upon whose bosom show has lain;
Who intimately lives with rain.

Poems are made by fools like me,
But only God can make a tree.

If—

Rudyard Kipling

If you can keep your head when all about you
    Are losing theirs and blaming it on you;
If you can trust yourself when all men doubt you
    But make allowance for their doubting too;
If you can wait and not be tired of waiting
    Or being lied about, don't deal in lies,
Or being hated, don't give way to hating,
    And yet don't look too good, nor talk too wise;

If you can dream—and make dreams your master;
    If you can think—and not make thoughts your aim;
If you can meet, with Triumph and Disaster
    And treat those two impostors just the same;
If you can bear to hear the truth you've spoken
    Twisted by knaves to make a trap for fools,
Or watch the things you gave your life to, broken,
    And stoop and build 'em up with worn-out tools;

If you can make one heap of all your winnings
    And risk it on one turn of pitch-and-toss,
And lose, and start again at your beginnings
    And never breathe a word about your loss;
If you can force your heart and nerve and sinew
    To serve your turn long after they are gone,
And so hold on when there is nothing in you
    Except the Will which says to them: 'Hold on!';

If you can talk with crowds and keep your virtue,
    Or walk with Kings—nor lose the common touch;
If neither foes nor loving friends can hurt you;
    If all men count with you, but none too much;
If you can fill the unforgiving minute
    With sixty seconds' worth of distance run,
Yours is the Earth and everything that's in it,
    And—which is more—you'll be a Man, my son!

The Alphabet

Arun Kolatkar

anvil arrow bow box brahmin
cart chariot cloud and compost heap
are all sitting in their separate squares

corn cup deer duck and frock
ganesh garlic hexagon and house
all have places of their own

inkpot jackfruit kite lemon and lotus
mango medicine mother old man and ostrich
are all holding their proper positions

pajamas pineapple rabbit and ram
sacrifice seal spoon and sugarcane
won't interfere with each other

47

swordtap tombstone and umbrella
warrior watermelon weight and yacht
have all found their eternal resting-place

the mother won't put her baby on the compost heap
the brahmin won't season the duck with garlic
the yacht won't hit the watermelon and sink

unless the ostrich eats the baby's frock
the warrior won't shoot an arrow into ganesh's belly
and if the ram doesn't knock down the old man

why would he need to smash the cup on the tombstone

At the Feet of a Child

For Emma-Maria, 1995
Rustum Kozain

The earth is young again tonight
And innocent of dinosaurs

Of war and famine; and small,
Cauled underneath a child.

Seven months, Emma rocks
On all small fours and belly

Rocks back and forth
Until her feet find traction

And, gurgling, she launches
Into her first crawl, sets us

And the earth in motion.

Pussikins

Kirsi Kunnas
Translated by Herbert Lomas

Rosebud mouth and silky fur:
Pussikins, well, look at her,
Sitting as proper pussies ought,
Far away in thought.

Thinks Pussikins: oh what a treat
If there might be
A Mouse Tree, like an apple tree,
With dangling baby mice to eat.

When it was tea, I'd give it a tap,
And down they'd plop for me to snap.

Then she'd munch each juicy mouse,
Warm inside her teatime house,
Pussikins, she would,
Rosy little bud.

Choosing a Name

Charles and Mary Lamb

I have got a newborn sister;
I was nigh the first that kissed her.
When the nursing woman brought her
To papa, his infant daughter,
How papa's dear eyes did glisten!
She will shortly be to christen:
And papa has made the offer,
I shall have the naming of her.

Now I wonder what would please her,
Charlotte, Julia, or Louisa.
Ann and Mary, they're too common;
Joan's too formal for a woman;
Jane's a prettier name beside;
But we had a Jane that died.
They would say, if 'twas Rebecca,
That she was a little Quaker.
Edith's pretty, but that looks
Better in old English books;
Ellen's left off long ago;
Blanche is out of fashion now.
None that I have named as yet
Are so good as Margaret.
Emily is neat and fine.
What do you think of Caroline?

How I'm puzzled and perplexed
What to choose or think of next!
I am in a little fever.
Lest the name that I shall give her
Should disgrace her or defame her,
I will leave papa to name her.

The Trees

Philip Larkin

The trees are coming into leaf
Like something almost being said;
The recent buds relax and spread,
Their greenness is a kind of grief.

Is it that they are born again
And we grow old? No, they die too.
Their yearly trick of looking new
Is written down in rings of grain.

Yet still the unresting castles thresh
In full-grown thickness every May.
Last year is dead, they seem to say,
Begin afresh, afresh, afresh.

The Ahkond of Swat

Edward Lear

Who, or why, or which, or what,
Is the Ahkond of Swat?

Is he tall or short, or dark or fair?
Does he sit on a stool or sofa or chair,
Or Squat,
The Ahkond of Swat?

Is he wise or foolish, young or old?
Does he drink his soup and his coffee cold,
Or Hot,
The Ahkond of Swat?

Does he sing or whistle, jabber or talk,
And when riding abroad, does he gallop or walk,
Or Trot,
The Ahkond of Swat?

Does he wear a turban, a fez or a hat?
Does he sleep on a mattress, a bed or a mat,
Or a Cot,
The Ahkond of Swat?

When he writes a copy in round-hand size,
Does he cross his t's and finish his i's
With a Dot,
The Ahkond of Swat?

Can he write a letter concisely clear,
Without a speck or a smudge or smear
Or Blot,
The Ahkond of Swat?

Do his people like him extremely well?
Or do they, whenever they can, rebel,
Or Plot,
At the Ahkond of Swat?

If he catches them then, either old or young,
Does he have them chopped in pieces or hung,
Or Shot,
The Ahkond of Swat?

Do his people prig in the lanes or park?
Or even at times, when days are dark,
Garotte?
Oh, the Ahkond of Swat?

Does he study the wants of his own dominion?
Or doesn't he care for public opinion,
A Jot,
The Ahkond of Swat?

To amuse his mind, do his people show him
Pictures, or anyone's last new poem,
Or What,
For the Ahkond of Swat?

At night if he suddenly screams and wakes,
Do they bring him only a few small cakes,
Or a Lot,
For the Ahkond of Swat?

Does he live on turnips, tea or tripe,
Does he like his shawl to be marked with a stripe,
Or a Dot,
The Ahkond of Swat?

Does he like to lie on his back in a boat
Like the lady who lived in that isle remote,
Shalott,
The Ahkond of Swat?

Is he quiet, or always making a fuss?
Is his steward a Swiss or a Swede or a Russ,
Or a Scot,
The Ahkond of Swat?

Does he like to sit by the calm, blue wave?
Or to sleep and snore in a dark green cave,
Or a Grott,
The Ahkond of Swat?

Does he drink small beer from a silver jug?
Or a bowl? or a glass? or a cup? or a mug?
Or a Pot,
The Ahkond of Swat?

Does he beat his wife with a gold-topped pipe,
When she lets the gooseberries grow too ripe,
Or Rot,
The Ahkond of Swat?

Does he wear a white tie when he dines with his friends,
And tie it neat in a bow with ends,
Or a Knot,
The Ahkond of Swat?

Does he like new cream, and hate mince pies?
When he looks at the sun, does he wink his eyes,
Or Not,
The Ahkond of Swat?

Does he teach his subjects to roast and bake?
Does he sail about on an inland lake,
In a Yacht,
The Ahkond of Swat?

Someone, or nobody knows I wot
Who or which or why or what
Is the Ahkond of Swat!

Kinky Hair Blues

Una Marson

Gwine find a beauty shop
Cause I ain't a belle.
Gwine find a beauty shop
Cause I ain't a lovely belle.
The boys pass me by,
They say I's not so swell.

See oder young gals
So slick and smart.
See dose oder young gals
So slick and smart.
I jes gwine die on de shelf
If I don't mek a start.

I hate dat ironed hair
And dat bleaching skin.
Hate dat ironed hair
And dat bleaching skin.
But I'll be all alone
If I don't fall in.

Lord 'tis you did gie me
All dis kinky hair.
'Tis you did gie me
All dis kinky hair,
And I don't envy gals
What got dose locks so fair.

I like me black face
And me kinky hair.
I like me black face
And me kinky hair.
But nobody loves dem,
I jes don't tink it's fair.

Now I's gwine press me hair
And bleach me skin.
I's gwine press me hair
And bleach me skin.
What won't a gal do
Some kind of man to win.

To His Coy Mistress

Andrew Marvell

Had we but world enough, and time,
This coyness, lady, were no crime.
We would sit down and think which way
To walk, and pass our long love's day;
Thou by the Indian Ganges' side
Shouldst rubies find; I by the tide
Of Humber would complain. I would
Love you ten years before the Flood;
And you should, if you please, refuse
Till the conversion of the Jews.
My vegetable love should grow
Vaster than empires, and more slow.
An hundred years should go to praise
Thine eyes, and on thy forehead gaze;
Two hundred to adore each breast,
But thirty thousand to the rest;
An age at least to every part,
And the last age should show your heart.
For, lady, you deserve this state,
Nor would I love at lower rate.

But at my back I always hear
Time's winged chariot hurrying near;
And yonder all before us lie
Deserts of vast eternity.

Thy beauty shall no more be found,
Nor, in thy marble vault, shall sound
My echoing song; then worms shall try
That long preserv'd virginity,
And your quaint honour turn to dust,
And into ashes all my lust.
The grave's a fine and private place,
But none I think do there embrace.

Now, therefore, while the youthful hue
Sits on thy skin like morning dew,
And while thy willing soul transpires
At every pore with instant fires,
Now let us sport us while we may;
And now, like am'rous birds of prey,
Rather at once our time devour,
Than languish in his slow-chapp'd power.
Let us roll all our strength, and all
Our sweetness, up into one ball;
And tear our pleasures with rough strife
Thorough the iron gates of life.
Thus, though we cannot make our sun
Stand still, yet we will make him run.

An Epilogue

John Masefield

I have seen flowers come in stony places
And kind things done by men with ugly faces,
And the gold cup won by the worst horse at the races,
So I trust, too.

A Lesson

Kevin McCann

Teacher paces out
The afternoon

Note this.

Note that.

Learn by heart
For Monday.

One child
Pounced on explains,
'Seagulls talk to me.'

A controlled burst
Of laughter
From the class—

'Oh yes,
And what do they say?'

'It's in seagull,'
The child replies,
Then adding patiently,
'And it's no good
In English—doesn't rhyme!'

More laughter,
But less this time.

The Tropics in New York

Claude McKay

Bananas ripe and green, and ginger root,
Cocoa in pods and alligator pears,
And tangerines and mangoes and grapefruit,
Fit for the highest prize at parish fairs.

Set in the window, bringing memories
Of fruit trees laden by low-singing rills,
Of dewy dawns, and mystical blue skies
In benediction over nun-like hills.

My eyes grew dim, and I could no more gaze;
A wave of longing through my body swept,
And, hungry for the old familiar ways,
I turned aside and bowed my head and wept.

Where Will the Next One Come From

Arvind Krishna Mehrotra

The next one will come from the air
It will be an overripe pumpkin
It will be the missing shoe

The next one will climb down
From the tree
When I'm asleep

The next one I will have to sow
For the next one I will have
To walk in the rain.

The next one I shall not write
It will rise like bread
It will be the curse coming home.

On Hearing a Symphony of Beethoven

Edna St Vincent Millay

Sweet sounds, oh, beautiful music, do not cease!
Reject me not into the world again.
With you alone is excellence and peace,
Mankind made plausible, his purpose plain.
Enchanted in your air benign and shrewd,
With limbs a-sprawl and empty faces pale,

The spiteful and the stingy and the rude
Sleep like the scullions in the fairy tale.

This moment is the best the world can give:
The tranquil blossom on the tortured stem.
Reject me not, sweet sounds; oh, let me live,
A city spell-bound under the ageing sun.
Music my rampart, and my only one.

Blake's Tyger—Revisited

Michaela Morgan

*On hearing that tigers in captivity can gradually lose their colour, losing
their camouflaging stripes and fading gradually to white.*

Tiger! Tiger! Turning white
In a cage just twice your height.
Six paces left, six paces right,
A long slow day, a longer night.

Tiger! Tiger! Dreaming still
Of the scent? The chase? The kill?
And now? No need. No place. No scope.
No space. No point. No hope.

Tiger! Tiger! Paces. Paces.
Once he flashed through open space.

His world once echoed to his roars.
Now he's quiet. He stares. He snores.

An inch of sky glimpsed through the bars.
A puddle. Concrete. Smells of cars.
He sniffs the air. He slumps. He sighs.
And stares and stares through jaundiced eyes.

From I Love My Matatu

Cecilia Muhoho

this is my matatu and i love my matatu

i shall fill it with
stacks of human beings to the brim
i shall make more money enough to pay for
the matatu loan
the matatu insurance
the profit . . .
not to mention my official and non-official pay

my matatu never gets full
there is always space
for one more
we all travel sealed standing, kneeling and bottoms up

the fat travellers have a tendency
to take up much more space
remind me to leave them out next time
tell them to take the bus

(A matatu is a Kenyan city minibus, legendary for cramming in as many
people—along with their baggage and often livestock—as is possible.)

Song of a Dream

Sarojini Naidu

Once in the dream of a night I stood
Lone in the light of a magical wood,
Soul-deep in visions that poppy-like sprang;
And spirits of Truth were the birds that sang,
And spirits of Love were the stars that glowed,
And spirits of Peace were the streams that flowed
In that magical wood in the land of sleep.

Lone in the light of that magical grove,
I felt the stars of the spirits of Love
Gather and gleam round my delicate youth,
And I heard the song of the spirits of Truth;
To quench my longing I bent me low
By the streams of the spirits of Peace that flow
In that magical wood in the land of sleep.

In Praise of Ironing

Pablo Neruda

Translated by Alistair Reid

Poetry is pure white. It emerges from water, covered with
    drops,
is wrinkled, all in a heap.
It has to be spread out, the skin of this planet,
has to be ironed out, the sea's whiteness;
and the hands keep moving, moving,
the holy surfaces are smoothed out, and that is how things
    are accomplished.
Every day, hands are creating the world,
fire is married to steel,
and canvas, linen, and cotton come back
from the skirmishings of the laundries,
and out of light a dove is born—
pure innocence returns out of the swirl.

Granny Granny Please Comb My Hair

Grace Nichols

Granny Granny
please comb my hair
you always take your time
you always take such care

You put me to sit on a cushion
between your knees
you rub a little coconut oil
parting gentle as a breeze

Mummy Mummy
she's always in a hurry—hurry rush
she pulls my hair
sometimes she tugs

But Granny
you have all the time in the world
and when you're finished
you always turn my head and say
'Now who's a nice girl.'

In My Country

Pitika Ntuli

In my country they jail you
For what they think you think.
My uncle once said to me:
They'll implant a microchip
In our minds
To flash our thoughts and dreams

On to a screen at John Vorster Square.
I was scared:
By day I guard my tongue
By night my dreams.

A Baby Antelope

Niyi Osundare

A baby antelope
Once asked her pensive mother:
   Tell me, mother,
   How does one count the teeth of a lion?

Futility

Wilfred Owen

Move him into the sun—
Gently its touch awoke him once,
At home, whispering of fields unsown.
Always it woke him, even in France,
Until this morning and this snow.
If anything might rouse him now
The kind old sun will know.
Think how it wakes the seeds—
Woke once the clays of a cold star.
Are limbs, so dear-achieved, are sides
Full-nerved, still warm, too hard to stir?

Was it for this the clay grew tall?
—O what made fatuous sunbeams toil
To break earth's sleep at all?

The Itch

K. Ayyappa Paniker

my first itch
came to squat on my right knee.
my last itch
leaned on my left knee.
shan't we scratch, o my people,
shan't we scratch?

some say
the world was born
of a divine itch.
others say
the lord himself
was born of an itch.
the disputationists!
all i know is this—
the pleasure
of scratching an itch.
all else
may be illusion,
but this is truth eternal.

Moral Tales for the Young

Dorothy Parker

Maude, the brightest of the sex,
Forged her daddy's name to checks,
Took them to the local banks,
Cashed them with a smile of thanks.
All the money came in handy—
Maudie was so fond of candy!
Weight she gained in way affrighting,
So she's given up her writing.

Save the money, when you forge;
Little ladies do not gorge.

Don, the little apple-cheek,
Sold his aunt's blue-ribbon peke,
Sneaked it out of Auntie's house,
Hidden in his sailor blouse.
Donald planned to spend his earnings,
Gratifying all his yearnings.
But the chance for pleasure slipped him,
For the doggie's buyer gypped him.

If they can't complete the deal,
Nicer children do not steal.

Dear Mum

Brian Patten

While you were out
a cup went and broke itself,
a crack appeared in the blue vase
your great-great granddad
brought back from Mr Ming in China.
Somehow, without me even turning on the tap,
the sink mysteriously overflowed.
A strange jam-stain,
about the size of a boy's hand,
appeared on the kitchen wall.
I don't think we will ever discover
exactly how the cat
managed to turn on the washing machine
(specially from the inside),
or how Sis's pet rabbit went and mistook
the waste-disposal unit for a burrow.
I can tell you I was scared when,
as if by magic,
a series of muddy footprints
appeared on the new white carpet.
I was being good
(honest)
but I think the house is haunted, so,
knowing you're going to have a fit,
I've gone over to Gran's for a bit.

Solitude

Alexander Pope

How happy he, who free from care
The rage of courts, and noise of towns;
Contented breathes his native air,
In his own grounds.

Whose herds with milk, whose fields with bread,
Whose flocks supply him with attire,
Whose trees in summer yield him shade,
In winter fire.

Blest! who can unconcern'dly find
Hours, days, and years slide swift away,
In health of body, peace of mind,
Quiet by day,

Sound sleep by night; study and ease
Together mix'd; sweet recreation,
And innocence, which most does please,
With meditation.

Thus let me live, unheard, unknown;
Thus unlamented let me dye;
Steal from the world, and not a stone
Tell where I lye.

Desperately Seeking India

G.J.V. Prasad

In Delhi
Without a visa
In Madras
An Aryan spy

Kashmir's no vacation
They tell me it's a nation
And Punjab wants to die

In Bombay
I'm an invader
In Assam
An exploiting trader

They would throw me
From the hills
Kick me
From the plains
I promise
Never
To mention India again

After I Came Back from Iceland

Sheenagh Pugh

After I came back from Iceland,
I couldn't stop talking. It was the light,
you see, the light and the air. I tried to put it
into poems, even, but you couldn't write

the waterfall on White River, blinding
and glacial, nor the clean toy town
with the resplendent harbour for its glass.
You couldn't write how the black lava shone,

nor how the outlines of the bright red roofs
cut the sky sharp as a knife; how breathing
was like drinking cold water. When I got back
to Heathrow and walked out into Reading,

I damn near choked on this warm gritty stuff
I called air; also on the conjecture
that we'd all settle for second best
once we'd forgotten there was something more.

Not Long Ago

Alisha Raghavan

Clothes you say
Must not be our only preoccupation
Friends you say
Must not be our only preoccupation

Forgetting to do our homework
You say is sinful
Keeping away from games field
You say is harmful

Junk food you say
Is abominable
Television you say
Is baneful

But not long ago
You too were a child like me.

Dove

Dahlia Ravikovitch

Once there was a white dove.
Oh love this dove.
She sprouted wings and flew from her nest.
Oh love this dove.

On her way she met the raven lord.
Oh love this dove.
On her way she met wolves in a horde.
Oh love this dove.

She met seventy-seven of the enemy.
Oh love this dove.
Other birds pecked her in envy.
Oh love this dove.

Lily-white till the day she was devoured.
Oh love this dove.
From a glimpse of her wings a legend flowered.
Oh love the white dove.

Discovery of India

Anushka Ravishankar

My cousin Nibboo—Boo for short
Once traversed India
South to North

At Parur he was very pleased
He said, 'I am—'
And then he sneezed

Srirangapatnam turned him soft
He sighed, 'I do—'
And then he coughed

At Wardha he was feeling well
He claimed, 'I can—'
And then he fell

In Meerut he was rather mild
He said, 'I will—'
And then he smiled

Ferozepur filled him with fear
He cried, 'I think!'
Then disappeared

Boo got famous overnight—
He proved Descartes
Wasn't right.

I Love You, I Tell Everyone

Mirkka Rekola

Translated by Herbert Lomas

My parents were anxious to sleep
When, as a child, I told them
Their bed was speeding through space—
You could see the stars tiny in the window
And their bed speeding along the pane.
They pulled the clothes over their heads
And turned their backs
Like the earth wanting a rest from the light.

My Point

Santan Rodrigues

father, in his paternal mood,
took utmost care
to advocate the good-
ness of life—all in neat,
easy-to-remember points.

mother always made it a point
to send me spick and span
to school. and sister dear
took care to point out
my language or ways
when either began to waver.
they all had a point.

wise guy, i
each day
pointed
the other way.

Hopping Frog

Christina Rossetti

Hopping frog, hop here and be seen,
I'll not pelt you with stick or stone.
Your cap is laced and your coat is green.
Goodbye, we'll let each other alone.

Traditional Children's Song

Translated by Chris Searle

If all the world's children
wanted to play holding hands
they could happily make
a wheel around the sea.

If all the world's children
wanted to play holding hands
they could be sailors
and build a bridge across the seas.

What a beautiful chorus we would make
singing around the earth
if all the humans in the world
wanted to dance holding hands!

Song from *The Tempest*

William Shakespeare

Full fathom five thy father lies;
Of his bones are coral made;
Those are pearls that were his eyes:
Nothing of him that doth fade,
But doth suffer a sea change
Into something rich and strange.
Sea-nymphs hourly ring his knell:
Hark! now I hear them—ding-dong, bell.

Sleep

Kriti Sharma

When I dug up the ground,
Mixed the soil
And put the seed in,
I wondered—
Would it be grateful to me
For breaking its sleep?

Lizard

Manohar Shetty

Tense, wizened,
Wrinkled neck twisting,
She clears
The air of small
Aberrations
With a snapping tongue,
A long tongue.

Ice Golawalla

Beheroze Shroff

In the May vacation
when heat shrivelled
our tongues to twigs,
we hunted for you
like Arabs for an oasis.

On schooldays
saved five paise bus fare,
walked home.
At the *naka*
stopped by your cart,
resting on four flattened tyres.
under our vulture eyes
your hands shaped

on a stick
a ball of ice shavings
on which you poured
red-coloured syrup.

Ice gola made our hearts
tinkle like the bell
on your cart,
that our throats
echoed in infection.

Cat

Melanie Silgardo

You curl into your mouth
Catscratch you fold
your claws inwards.
Cold world of purr and fur.
All plans are clandestine.
Night thief. Lover in the dark.
United silhouette on the rooftop.
Careful confident master.
You start your climactic wail
growing in possibility
till it cracks the windowpane
and pads off into the cool black.
Catnap.

Tenuous and Precarious

Stevie Smith

Tenuous and Precarious
Were my guardians,
Precarious and Tenuous,
Two Romans.

My father was Hazardous,
Hazardous,
Dear old man,
Three Romans.

There was my brother Spurious,
Spurious Posthumous,
Spurious was Spurious,
Was four Romans.

My husband was Perfidious,
He was Perfidious,
Five Romans.

Surreptitious, our son,
Was Surreptitious,
He was six Romans.

Our cat Tedious
Still lives,
Count not Tedious
Yet.

My name is Finis,
Finis, Finis,
I am Finis,
Six, five, four, three, two,
One Roman,
Finis.

The Key

Fatou Ndiaye Sow

Translated by Véronique Tadjo

My child, my hope,
Everything in nature
Speaks to you:
The sun, the moon,
The bird
Which flies by,
The river which flows
And even the cold stone;
If you know
How to listen, look and feel,
You will find the key to the universe.

Block City

Robert Louis Stevenson

What are you able to build with your blocks?
Castles and palaces, temples and docks.
Rain may keep raining, and others go roam,
But I can be happy and building at home.

Let the sofa be mountains, the carpet be sea,
There I'll establish a city for me:
A kirk and a mill and a palace beside,
And a harbour as well where my vessels may ride.

Great is the palace with pillar and wall,
A sort of a tower on top of it all,
And steps coming down in an orderly way
To where my toy vessels lie safe in the bay.
This one is sailing and that one is moored:
Hark to the song of the sailors on board!
And see on the steps of my palace, the kings
Coming and going with presents and things!

A Small Poem for My Father
While Waiting for a Long
and Extended Conversation
Which Very Probably
Will Never Take Place

Nicolás Suescún

With you I can't talk
about anything
even though my eyes
and my nose be yours
—as they've told me—
or that I have been
your greatest mistake
—so they've suggested—
and that, in a certain way,
it's you, not me, who walks
—which is what I suspect—
when I walk on the street.

From Verses on the Death of Dr Swift

Jonathan Swift

Had he but spar'd his Tongue and Pen,
He might have rose like other Men:
But, Power was never in his Thought;
And, Wealth he valu'd not a Groat:
Ingratitude he often found,
And pity'd those who meant the Wound:
But kept the Tenor of his Mind,
To merit well of human Kind:
Nor made a Sacrifice of those
Who still were true, to please his Foes.
He labour'd many a fruitless Hour
To reconcile his Friends in Power;
Saw Mischief by a Faction brewing,
While they pursu'd each others Ruin.
But, finding vain was all his Care,
He left the Court in mere Despair.

Where the Mind is without Fear

Rabindranath Tagore

Where the mind is without fear and the head is held high
Where knowledge is free
Where the world has not been broken up into fragments
By narrow domestic walls
Where words come out from the depth of truth
Where tireless striving stretches its arms towards perfection
Where the clear stream of reason has not lost its way
Into the dreary desert sand of dead habit
Where the mind is led forward by thee
Into ever-widening thought and action
Into that heaven of freedom, my Father, let my country awake

The Charge of the Light Brigade

Alfred Lord Tennyson

Half a league, half a league,
Half a league onward,
All in the valley of death
Rode the six hundred.
'Charge,' was the captain's cry;
Their's not to reason why,
Their's not to make reply,
Their's but to do and die,
Into the valley of Death
Rode the six hundred.

Cannon to right of them,
Cannon to left of them,
Cannon in front of them
Volley'd and thunder'd;
Storm'd at with shot and shell,
Boldly they rode and well;
Into the jaws of Death,
Into the mouth of Hell,
Rode the six hundred.

Flash'd all their sabres bare,
Flash'd all at once in air,
Sabring the gunners there,
Charging an army, while

All the world wonder'd:
Plunged in the battery-smoke
Fiercely the line they broke;
Strong was the sabre-stroke;
Making an army reel
Shaken and sunder'd.
Then they rode back, but not,
Not the six hundred.

Cannon to right of them,
Cannon to left of them,
Cannon behind them
Volley'd and thunder'd;
Storm'd at with shot and shell,
They that had struck so well
Rode thro' the jaws of Death,
Half a league back again,
Up from the mouth of Hell,
All that was left of them,
left of six hundred.

Honour the brave and bold!
Long shall the tale be told,
Yea, when our babes are old—
How they rode onward.

Exile House

Tenzin Tsundue

Our tiled roof dripped
and the four walls threatened to fall apart
but we were to go home soon,
we grew papayas
in front of our house
chillies in our garden
and *changmas* for our fences,
then pumpkins rolled down the cowshed thatch
calves trotted out of the manger,
grass on the roof,
beans sprouted and
climbed down the vines,
money plants crept in through the window,
our house seems to have grown roots.
The fences have grown into a jungle,
now how can I tell my children
where we came from?

A Kind of War

Raeesa Vakil

There is no screaming of guns,
But instead a squealing of chainsaws.
The ground will not later be wet with blood,
But will be parched without water.

Sickening wounds will not greet your eyes,
But the aching stumps of trees.
Fruits will be gritty in your mouth.

The Cyber River

Shreekumar Varma

hacking through forests of deadly data
and backing-up each of them later,
I suffered a dangerous virus sting
but resumed with infinite zip and zing.

thick foliage of pop-ups and banners
and sudden beasts with really no manners;
I crawled and I crept and I plodded on
to places no nerd had then trodded on.

I stole through a game that won me a prize,
though it's really the steal that gave me the highs.
but, hush! there's this department site
that honestly gave me a terrible fright.

the squeak and the roar and the howl of a hound,
though I'd taken great care to lower the sound.
I'm nearing the end, I've forded a creek—
jolly adventurer, no more a geek!

I type in a name and the shrubbery parts:
see there's a sight to warm up your hearts!

sipping the sun in a silver repast
the river that crosses your future and past!

dressed in a smile I dive in so fast
that even the fish are rather aghast;
there's nothing on earth that can ever compare
with the synthetic waves of a million software!

I swim and I leap and I frolic about,
I already feel I'll never get out!
the earth and the sky and a golden sunlight
are nothing compared to the cyber delight!

they're calling me now as they generally do
but soon they will tire of all this ado,
they'll leave me alone and go back to bed
the waters are closing just over my head.

You Cannot Hope

Humbert Wolfe

You cannot hope
to bribe or twist,
thank God! the
British journalist.

But, seeing what
the man will do
unbribed, there's
no occasion to.

My Heart Leaps Up

William Wordsworth

My heart leaps up when I behold
    A rainbow in the sky:
So was it when my life began;
So is it now I am a man;
So be it when I shall grow old,
    Or let me die!
The Child is father of the Man;
And I could wish my days to be
Bound each to each by natural piety.

The Little Clock

Elinor Wylie

Half-past-four and the first bird waking,
Falling on my heart like a thin green leaf.
If you are alive, your heart is breaking,
If you are dead, you are done with grief
Half-past-five and the birds singing sweetly,
World washed silver with the rain and the wind.
If you are a saint, you have lived discreetly,
If you are a sinner, you have surely sinned.
Half-past-seven and the birds singing madly;
Sun flames up in the sky like a lark.
If there are things to remember sadly,
Wait and remember them after dark.

A Hot Day

Arthur Yap

On a hot day I think
Everything is an accident
And things being what they aren't
I have sometimes stood along
Corridors and seen the world
Spinning on its axis

And the child's distant balloon
Is a little globe
Attached to a string
With the bigger blue balloon
Of the sky stretched behind

The Lake Isle of Innisfree

W.B. Yeats

I will arise and go now, and go to Innisfree,
And a small cabin build there, of clay and wattles made:
Nine bean-rows will I have there, a hive for the honeybee,
And live alone in the bee-loud glade.

And I shall have some peace there, for peace comes
    dropping slow,
Dropping from the veils of the morning to where the
    cricket sings;
There midnight's all a glimmer, and noon a purple glow,
And evening full of the linnet's wings.

I will arise and go now, for always night and day
I hear lake water lapping with low sounds by the shore;
While I stand on the roadway, or on the pavements grey,
I hear it in the deep heart's core.

Acknowledgements

The editors and the publishers would like to thank the following for permission to reprint copyright material:

The poet for 'The Discovery of India' by Anushka Ravishankar;

The poet for 'A Hot Day' by Arthur Yap, from *The Second Tongue* (Singapore: Heinemann), edited by Edwin Thumboo;

The poet for 'The Alphabet' by Arun Kolatkar, originally written in Marathi and published in *Arun Kolatkarachya Kavita* (Mumbai: Pras Prakashan);

The poet for 'Where Will the Next One Come From' from *Middle Earth* (Delhi: Oxford University Press) by Arvind Krishna Mehrotra;

The poet for 'Ice Golawalla' by Beheroze Shroff;

Bloodaxe Books for 'A Boy's Head' from *Selected Poems* (London: Bloodaxe) by Miroslav Holub, translated by Ian Milner and 'For a Five Year Old' from *Poems* by Fleur Adcock;

The poet for 'I Love My Matatu' by Cecilia Muhoho;

The poet for 'No, Sir, I Do Not Wish to Remain in the USA' from *A Spelling Guide to Women* (Hyderabad: Orient Longman) by Charmayne D'Souza;

The translator for 'Traditional Children's Song' translated by Chris Searle, from *Free My Mind: An Anthology of Black and*

Asian Poetry (London: Hamish Hamilton), edited by Judith Elkin and Carlton Duncan;

David Higham Associates for 'What Has Happened to Lulu?' from *Collected Poems 1951–2000* (London: Macmillan) by Charles Causley;

Dee Jarrett-Macauley for 'Kinky Hair Blues' by Una Marson from *The Penguin Book of Caribbean Verse* (London: Penguin), edited by Paula Burnett;

The poet for 'Women on the Road to Lhasa' from *Do Not Weep Lonely Mirror* (Mumbai: Frog Books) by Deepa Agarwal;

The poet for 'Pahari Parrots' from *Dangerlok* (Delhi: Penguin) by Eunice de Souza;

Faber and Faber for 'Macavity: The Mystery Cat' from *Old Possum's Book of Practical Cats* (London: Faber) by T.S. Eliot, 'Night Mail' from *Collected Poems* (London: Faber) by W.H. Auden, and 'The Trees' (London: Faber) from *Collected Poems* by Philip Larkin;

Farrar, Straus and Giroux for 'In Praise of Ironing' from *Fully Empowered* (New York: FSG) by Pablo Neruda, translated by Alistair Reid;

Gerald Duckworth & Co. Ltd for 'Moral Tales for the Young' from *The Uncollected Dorothy Parker* (London: Duckworth) by Dorothy Parker;

The poet for 'Granny Granny Please Comb My Hair' by Grace Nichols from *I Like That Stuff* (Cambridge: Cambridge University Press), edited by Morag Styles;

Hamish MacGibbon, James and James for 'Tenuous and Precarious' from *The Collected Poems of Stevie Smith* (London: James MacGibbon) by Stevie Smith;

Haranand Publications for 'Desperately Seeking India' from *In Delhi without a Visa* (Delhi: Haranand) by G.J.V. Prasad;

The editor for 'I Love You, I Tell Everyone' by Mirkka Rekola and 'Pussikins' by Kirsi Kunnas from *Contemporary Finnish Poetry* (London: Bloodaxe), edited by Herbert Lomas;

The poet for 'A Parent's/Child's Poem' from *The Man in the Dark Glasses* (Mumbai: St Xavier's College) by Jimmy P. Avasia;

The poet for 'The Itch' by K. Ayyappa Paniker;

The poet for 'A Lesson' by Kevin McCann from *Beyond Bedlam* (London: Anvil Press), edited by Ken Smith and Matthew Sweeney;

The poet for 'I am Becoming My Mother' from *I Am Becoming My Mother* (London: New Beacon Books) by Lorna Goodison;

The poet for 'Made for Each Other' from *Tribute to Papa and Other Poems* (Kolkata: Writer's Workshop) by Mamta Kalia;

The poet for 'Lizard' from *Domestic Creatures* (Delhi: Oxford University Press) by Manohar Shetty;

Mark Bostridge and Rebecca Williams, literary executors for the estate of Vera Brittain, for 'To My Brother' from *Verses of a VAD* (London: Erskine MacDonald) by Vera Brittain;

The poet for 'Cats' by Melanie Silgardo from *Skies of Design* (London: College of Printing);

The poet for 'Blake's Tyger—Revisited' from *Through the Window* (London: Longman) by Michaela Morgan;

The poet for 'A Small Poem for My Father' from *La vida es* (Bogota: Universidad Nacional de Colombia) by Nicolás Suescún;

The poet for 'A Baby Antelope' from *Waiting Laughters* (Lagos: Malthouse Press) by Niyi Osundare;

Pearson Educational Australia for 'Homecoming' from *Sometimes Gladness* (Melbourne: Pearson Educational) by Bruce Dawe;

Penguin Books UK for 'Dear Mum' from *Thawing Frozen Frogs* (London: Viking) by Brian Patten;

Persis Anklesaria and the poet for 'Injection' from *Family Sunday and Other Poems* (Mumbai: Peacock Publishers) by Kavita Ezekiel;

The poet for 'In My Country' by Pitika Ntuli;

Random House Group UK for 'Rat Race' from *We Animals Would Like a Word with You* (London: Red Fox) by John Agard;

The poet for 'Cat' from *Apricot* by Rex Baker;

The poet for 'My Point' by Santan Rodrigues from *Three Poets* (Mumbai: Newground) by Melanie Silgardo, Raul D'Gama Rose and Rodrigues;

Seren Books for 'After I Came Back from Iceland' from *Selected Poems* (Bridgend: Seren Books) by Sheenagh Pugh;

Sheil Land Associates for 'Picnic in Jammu' from *Jets from Oranges* (London: Macmillan) by Zulfikar Ghose;

The poet for 'The Cyber River' by Shreekumar Varma;

The poet for 'Exile House' from *Kora* by Tenzin Tsundue;

The Institute for the Translation of Hebrew Literature for 'Palestinians' by Eli Alon and 'Dove' by Dahlia Ravikovitch from *A Chance Beyond Bombs* (Delhi: Penguin), edited by Haya Hoffman;

The Rishi Valley School for 'Sleep' by Kriti Sharma, 'A Kind of War' by Raeesa Vakil, 'Celebrations' by Ishan Agarwal, and 'Not Long Ago' by Alisha Raghavan (these poems were written at a poetry workshop conducted by Gieve Patel);

The Society of Authors as literary representatives of the estates of A.E. Housman, John Masefield and Walter de la Mare for 'Amelia Mixed the Mustard' by A.E. Housman, 'An Epilogue' by John Masefield and 'Kiph' by Walter de la Mare;

The Trustees of the Mrs Frances Crofts Cornford Deceased Will Trust for 'All Souls' Night' from *Collected Poems* (London: Enitharmon Press) by Frances Cornford;

The University of California Press for 'Children Going to School' by Hem Hamal from *Himalayan Voices* (Berkeley: University of California Press), translated and edited by Michael James Hutt;

Time Warner Books for 'On Ageing' from *The Complete Collected Works of Maya Angelou* (London: Virago) by Maya Angelou;

The translator for 'The Key' by Fatou Ndiaye Sow from *Chansons Pour Lalty* (Dakar: Les Nouvelles Editions Africaines), translated by Véronique Tadjo;

W.W. Norton & Co. for 'in Just-/ spring' from *Complete Poems 1904–1962* (London: Norton) by e.e. cummings, edited by George J. Firmage. Copyright © 1991 by the Trustees for the E.E. Cummings Trust and George James Firmage;

The Good Reading Guide for Children
Introduction by Ruskin Bond

Everything you wanted to know about books for children, but didn't know whom to ask!

A comprehensive guide to fiction in English for readers aged four to sixteen, *The Good Reading Guide for Children*

- is divided into three sections to suit every age group
- has entries listing over 1000 books
- is divided into categories with cross-references so that children can read more in genres they like
- includes classics as well as the best of contemporary works
- includes books from all over the world.

With an introduction by Ruskin Bond, India's best-known children's writer in English, *The Good Reading Guide* is an invaluable resource for children who love books, as well as for parents and friends looking for the right book for the young people in their lives.

The Elephant's Child and Other Stories: The Delightful World of Rudyard Kipling
Sudhakar Marathe

An enchanting collection of classic stories

How did the elephant get his long trunk? What happened when the little butterfly stamped in anger? How did the dog, horse and cow become man's first friends? Who wrote the first letter and invented the alphabet? In this collection of well-loved tales by Rudyard Kipling, we read of many such wonderful happenings. There are stories here from the *Jungle Book*, about Mowgli and his friends Baloo and Bagheera, and about Rikki-Tikki Tavi the brave mongoose. Also included are some of Kipling's stories about children, from *Just-So Stories*, *Plain Tales from the Hills* and elsewhere—featuring the irrepressible Tods, the charming Lispeth and creative little Muhammad Din.

For those who have read these stories earlier, this book contains some old favourites as well as some unusual ones; and for those reading Rudyard Kipling's stories for the first time, this is the perfect introduction to a world that is witty and imaginative, sensitive and rollickingly funny.

A Skyful of Stories: How the Constellations Came to Be
Shobha Viswanath

Tales from around the world of how the stars came to be

The night sky has always fascinated mankind. It has been a source of countless tales and legends, of omens and harbingers, of mysteries and enigmas.

Through the ages, several stories have been woven around the shapes and patterns that stars form in the night sky. Various cultures from around the world have contributed to these stories. From the great classics of Greece, Rome and ancient India to tales from Egyptian, aboriginal, Asian and Native American traditions, these accounts are fascinating interpretations of how the constellations came to be associated with concepts and ideas that are so human.

Shobha Viswanath gathers together the stories behind the origins of stars as well as those behind seven constellations—Ursa Major, Ursa Minor, Orion, Pleiades, Aries, Canis Major and Centaurus. *A Skyful of Stories* puts faces on the stars so that the next time you gaze at the night skies, it will be peopled with characters you know and love.

From Bugs to Black Holes: Discoveries That Changed the World
Shobhit Mahajan

Did you know that...

- The first alarm clock could ring only at 4 a.m.?
- Isaac Newton spent his later years trying to transform base metals into gold?
- The last samples of the smallpox virus are kept in two secret laboratories in Siberia and in the US?
- John Dalton, who formulated the theory of the atom, started running a school at the age of twelve?
- Charles Babbage, who invented the first computer, once baked himself in an oven?
- The world's first telephone directory was a single sheet of paper with fifty names?

We take so many things for granted today: we have clocks that show the time; electric lights; music on the radio; telephone conversations with friends; work on our computers; antibiotics that cure us when we are ill. But even as recently as 150 years ago, many of these things were not available or possible. This fascinating book examines twenty concepts and things that have transformed our lives and the way we live. It looks at the thought behind these ideas and inventions, and the people who finally pulled it all together.

Inspirational, funny, irreverent, and filled with fascinating facts and memorable stories, *From Bugs to Black Holes* is a look at some of the amazing people in different times whose ideas have shaped the way we live today.